Smithsonian Prehistoric Zone

Stegosaurus

by Gerry Bailey
Illustrated by Karen Carr

Crabtree Publishing Company

www.crabtreebooks.com

Crabtree Publishing Company
www.crabtreebooks.com

Author
Gerry Bailey

Illustrator
Karen Carr

Editorial coordinator
Kathy Middleton

Editor
Lynn Peppas

Proofreaders
Reagan Miller
Kathy Middleton

Prepress technician
Samara Parent

Print and production coordinator
Katherine Berti

Copyright © 2010 Palm Publishing LLC and the
Smithsonian Institution, Washington DC, 20560 USA
All rights reserved.

Stegosaurus, originally published as *A Busy Day for Stegosaurus*
by Dawn Bentley, Illustrated by Karen Carr
Book copyright © 2003 Trudy Corporation and the Smithsonian
Institution, Washington DC 20560.

Library of Congress Cataloging-in-Publication Data

Bailey, Gerry.
  Stegosaurus / by Gerry Bailey ; illustrated by Karen Carr
    p. cm. -- (Smithsonian prehistoric zone)
  Includes index.
  ISBN 978-0-7787-1816-1 (pbk. : alk. paper) -- ISBN 978-0-7787-1803-1
(reinforced library binding : alk. paper) -- ISBN 978-1-4271-9707-8
(electronic (pdf))
  1. Stegosaurus--Juvenile literature. I. Carr, Karen, 1960- , ill. II. Title.

  QE862.O65B346 2011
  567.915'3--dc22
                        2010044032

Library and Archives Canada Cataloguing in Publication

Bailey, Gerry
  Stegosaurus / by Gerry Bailey ; illustrated by Karen Carr.

(Smithsonian prehistoric zone)
Includes index.
At head of title: Smithsonian Institution.
Issued also in electronic format.
ISBN 978-0-7787-1803-1 (bound).--ISBN 978-0-7787-1816-1 (pbk.)

  1. Stegosaurus--Juvenile literature. I. Carr, Karen, 1960-
II. Smithsonian Institution III. Title. IV. Series: Bailey, Gerry.
Smithsonian prehistoric zone.

  QE862.O65B337 2011   j567.915'3   C2010-906890-4

Published in the United States
Crabtree Publishing
PMB 59051
350 Fifth Avenue, 59th Floor
New York, New York 10118

Published in Canada
Crabtree Publishing
616 Welland Ave.
St. Catharines, Ontario
L2M 5V6

Printed in China/012011/GW20101014

Dinosaurs

Living things had been around for billions of years before dinosaurs came along. Animal life on Earth started with single-cell **organisms** that lived in the seas. About 380 million years ago, some animals came out of the sea and onto the land. These were the ancestors that would become the mighty dinosaurs.

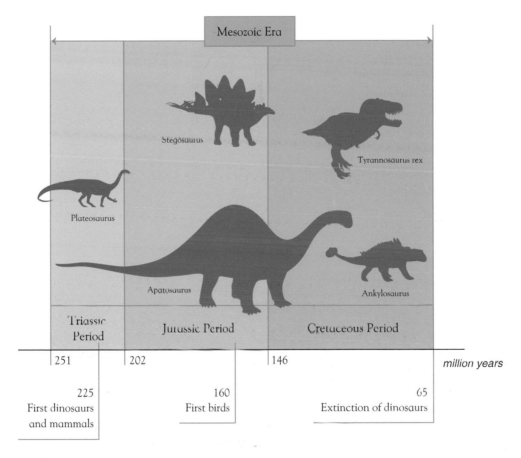

Mesozoic Era

Stegosaurus

Tyrannosaurus rex

Plateosaurus

Apatosaurus

Ankylosaurus

Triassic Period | Jurassic Period | Cretaceous Period

| 251 | 202 | 146 | *million years* |

225
First dinosaurs
and mammals

160
First birds

65
Extinction of dinosaurs

The dinosaur era is called the Mesozoic era. It is divided into three parts called the Triassic, Jurassic, and Cretaceous periods. During the Jurassic period the climate was warm and plenty of rain fell. Plant-eating dinosaurs, such as *Stegosaurus*, fed on ferns, horsetails, cycad leaves, and pinecones. Meat-eaters, such as *Allosaurus*, fed on the plant-eaters and other dinosaurs. Most dinosaurs (except birds) had been wiped out by the end of the Cretaceous period. No one is sure exactly why.

Stegosaurus had been guarding her eggs during
the cool night. She had stayed very still through
the night. Her whole body was chilly. She needed
to get warm now that morning had come.

She walked into the sunlight so that the plates standing up along her back could catch the sun's rays. These plates were covered in blood-rich skin and soon her whole body was warm.

Stegosaurus had to eat now that she felt
warmer. She needed a lot of food to make
energy for her huge body. Her powerful back
legs were twice as long as her front legs.

She could easily find food on the
ground. She could also lift her front
legs to tear leaves from the lower
branches of trees.

Stegosaurus snipped off a piece of fern using her horny beak. She had no teeth in the front of her jaws and only weak ones in her cheeks. For this reason, she could not chew her food. She swallowed the plants whole.

She may have swallowed small
stones to help her **digest**. The
stones would help her to grind
up the food in her stomach.

Stegosaurus looked for more food as she **plodded** along on her great legs. She could not move quickly because her legs were built for strength, to carry her huge body. Her front legs were short and gave her a plodding movement. Tiny animals had to **beware** as she lowered her great feet.

Stegosaurus needed to drink.
She stopped at a stream.
She had to be careful at
the stream.

Sometimes a mighty meat-eating Allosaurus
lurked nearby waiting to pounce on thirsty
prey. Stegosaurus was not fast enough to
escape such a frightening **predator.**

Other dinosaurs had come to the stream to drink and splash. A tall plant-eating Brachiosaurus stayed to drink a little. It lifted its long neck to nibble tender leaves from the top of a nearby tree.

Suddenly, Stegosaurus lifted her head.
She had heard the frightened cry of a tiny,
feathered **carnivore** called Coeleurosaur.
This was a sure sign that danger was close by.

Just then, an Allosaurus charged out of the trees. Its teeth were bared. Stegosaurus was too slow to get away. She defended herself by turning her back to it. As Allosaurus loomed above her, Stegosaurus swung her tail.

It was armed at its tips with pairs of long,
sharp spikes. It was a fearful weapon.
Allosaurus swerved away as Stegosaurus
swung her tail dangerously from side to side.

Allosaurus moved in again. It tore at Stegosaurus
with the sharp claws on its hand. The bony bumps
on Stegosaurus's skin protected her. She only
received a small scratch.

Stegosaurus swung her tail with even more force.
It struck the meat-eater and sent it sprawling.
Allosaurus was injured. It gave Stegosaurus
enough time to make her escape.

It was midday now and Stegosaurus was hot from the fight and from the fierce sun overhead. She found a cool place to rest in the shade of a tree.

The plates along her back would now help to
cool her blood. She would search for food again
after she had rested and cooled down.

Stegosaurus made her way toward a patch of
ferns. There was something there ahead of her.
It was a fierce-looking **armored** Gargoyleosaurus.
It was chomping away at the ferns.

This smaller dinosaur was peaceful and there were plenty of ferns to share. The land was covered with lush **tropical** vegetation. At that time, plant-eaters such as these could eat well.

Now it was time to return to her nest. Stegosaurus was happy to see that several of the eggs had hatched and the baby dinosaurs were well. They did not look like their mother at this stage.

They had no plates on their backs. Plates
would grow as the babies got older.
Stegosaurus made sure there was no danger
lurking nearby and settled down to sleep.

All about Stegosaurus

(STEG-oh-SAW-russ)

Stegosaurus lived during the late Jurassic period around 155 to 145 million years ago. Its name means "roof lizard." It was a herbivore, which means it ate only plants.

Stegosaurus weighed around 2.2 tons (2 metric tons) and grew up to 30 feet (9 meters) long. Its huge back legs were twice the length of its front ones, so it sloped forward from its hips. It was a big dinosaur. But its head was very small compared to the rest of its body. A *Stegosaurus* head measured about 18 inches (45 centimeters). It contained a small brain about the size of a walnut. This means it probably was not very intelligent. It did not need to be because it did not have to chase other dinosaurs to get food.

At the front of its jaws, *Stegosaurus* had a toothless beak. It also had a set of small teeth along its cheeks but these could only be used for chopping soft plants. *Stegosaurus* probably swallowed stones to help digest its food. The stones stayed in its stomach to help grind down plant material.

Stegosaurus had two lines of leaf-shaped bony plates along its back. They started from just behind its head to half way down its tail. At first, **paleontologists** thought the plates might be used as a kind of defense to protect the dinosaur's back. Now, most believe that they were also used to help control body temperature. The plates were covered in skin that held a large supply of blood. The blood near the surface of the skin would be warmed by the sun, or cooled if the dinosaur moved into the shade. The warmed or cooled blood would be pumped around its body as a kind of temperature control.

Stegosaurus had two pairs of spikes about three feet (1 meter) long at the end of its tail. It would have used these sharp, horn-covered spikes to defend itself. It could swipe at any attackers by swinging its tail from side to side.

Period	Permian Period	Triassic Period	Jurassic Period	Cretaceous Period			

248

Mesozoic Era

65

Cenozoic Era

Now

1.8
First humans

Stegosaur family

All the members of the *stegosaur* family had **distinctive** small heads and large bodies. They also had a row of bony plates that grew down either side of the animal's backbone.

Stegosaurs, such as *Kentrosaurus*, *Tuojiangosaurus*, *Wuerhosaurus*, and *Stegosaurus*, may have lived in herds. *Tuojiangosaurus* and *Wuerhosaurus* both lived in what is now China.

Name: *Kentrosaurus*
Family: Stegosaur
Time: Late Jurassic
Size: 16 feet (5 meters)
Location: Africa

Name: *Tuojiangosaurus*
Family: Stegosaur
Time: Late Jurassic
Size: 23 feet (7 meters)
Location: China

Name: Wuerhosaurus
Family: Stegosaur
Time: Early Cretaceous
Size: 20 feet (6 meters)
Location: China

Name: *Stegosaurus*
Family: Stegosaur
Time: Late Jurassic
Size: 30 feet (9 meters)
Location: North America

Dinosaur brains

Most dinosaurs were not very intelligent but some were probably smarter than others. Scientists calculate how intelligent a dinosaur was by measuring its brain size compared to its body weight. This is called its *EQ*, which stands for *Encephalization Quotient*.

Hip Nerve Pocket

Stegosaurus had a small brain compared to its size, so it is not far up the *EQ* chart. It measured just over 0.5. Its brain was probably the size of a walnut. It did, however, have a sort of "relay center" for nerve signals where the nerves of the hips and hind feet meet. While this did not contain brain tissue, it did make *Stegosaurus* more complex than its brain size would suggest.

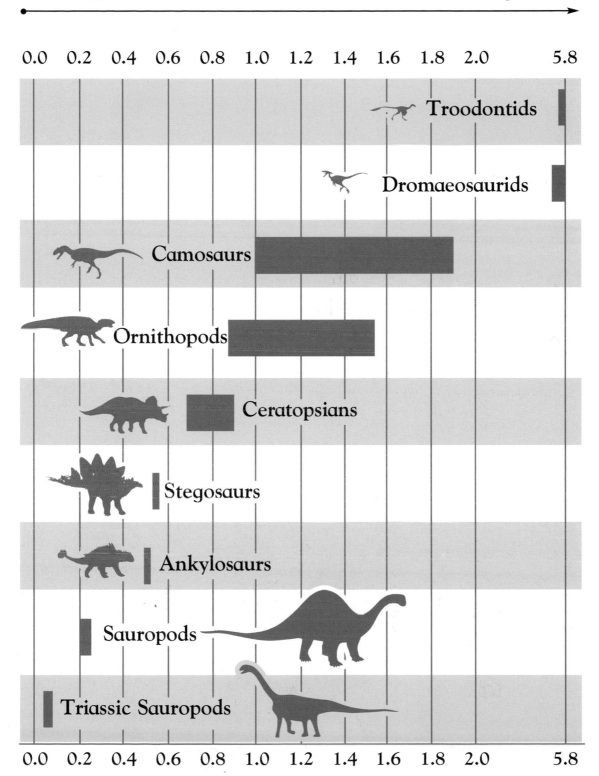

lowest EQ   highest EQ

0.0 0.2 0.4 0.6 0.8 1.0 1.2 1.4 1.6 1.8 2.0   5.8

Troodontids

Dromaeosaurids

Camosaurs

Ornithopods

Ceratopsians

Stegosaurs

Ankylosaurs

Sauropods

Triassic Sauropods

0.0 0.2 0.4 0.6 0.8 1.0 1.2 1.4 1.6 1.8 2.0   5.8

Glossary

armor A thick, protective layer of bone just under the skin

beware To watch out for

carnivore An animal that eats the flesh of other animals

digest To break down and change food so that it can be absorbed by the body

distinctive Having a different or special characteristic that others do not have

organisms Any living plant or animal

paleontologist A scientist who studies prehistoric life such as dinosaurs

plod To walk heavily and slowly

predator An animal that hunts other animals for food

prey An animal that is hunted by another animal

tropical An area where the climate is usually hot and humid

vertebrae Bones that make up the spinal column

Index

Further Reading and Websites

Stegosaurus Up Close by Peter Dodson. Enslow Publishers (2010)

Stegosaurus by Helen Greathead. Scholastic (2010)

Websites:

www.smithsonianeducation.org